GLEN ROUNDS was born in the Badlands of South Dakota and spent his boyhood on a ranch in Montana. Later, he traveled around the country as a sign painter, cowpuncher, mule skinner, carnival barker, and logger. He studied at the Kansas City Art Institute, the Art Students' League in New York, and served in the U.S. Army. Mr. Rounds is the author of many books for young readers and lives in Southern Pines, North Carolina.

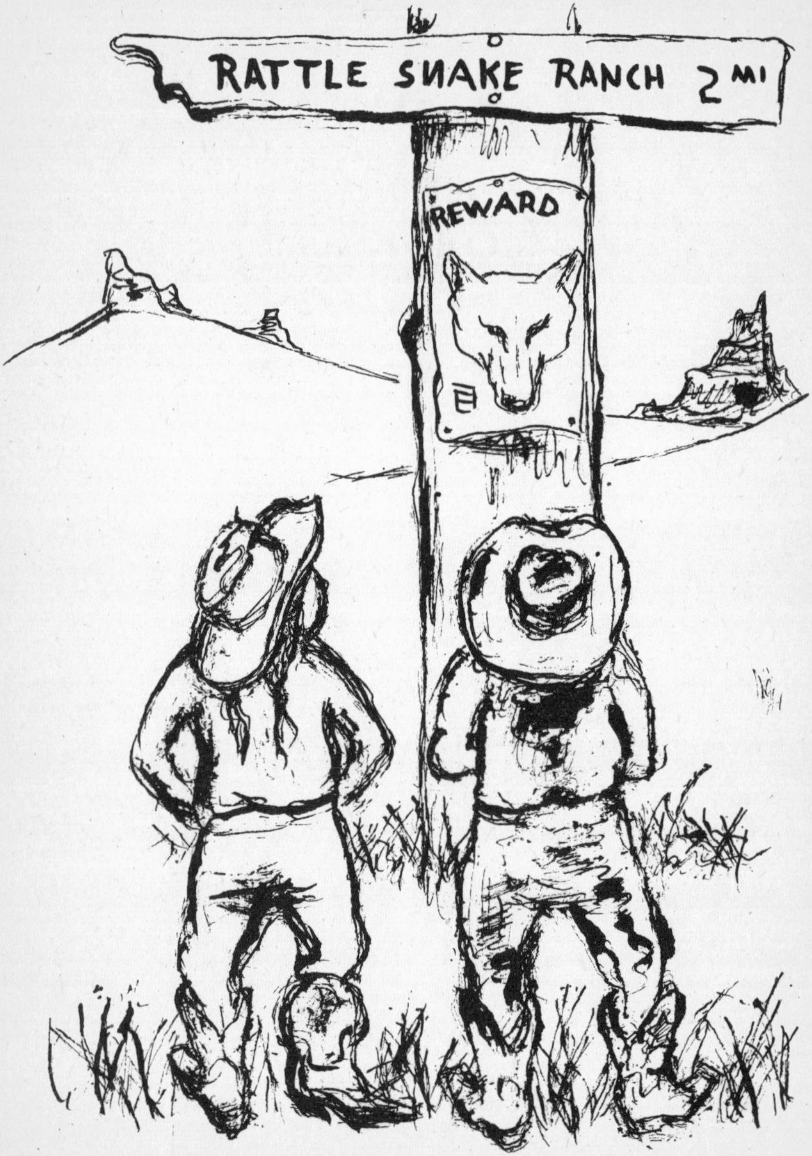
RATTLE SNAKE RANCH 2 MI
REWARD

WHITEY
AND THE COLT-KILLER

Written and Illustrated by

Glen Rounds

AN AVON CAMELOT BOOK

6th grade reading level has been determined by using the Fry Readability Scale.

AVON BOOKS
A division of
The Hearst Corporation
959 Eighth Avenue
New York, New York 10019

Copyright © 1962 by Glen Rounds
Cover illustration by Murray Tinkelman
Published by arrangement with Holiday House, Inc.
Library of Congress Catalog Card Number: 81-20502
ISBN: 0-380-57158-7

First Camelot Printing, May, 1982

Library of Congress Cataloging in Publication Data

Rounds, Glen, 1906-
    Whitey and the colt-killer.

    (An Avon/Camelot Book)
    Originally published: New York: Holiday
House, 1962.
    Summary: Whitey and his cousin Josie set
off to capture an old wolf that's been
injuring colts. [1. Ranch life—Fiction]
I. Title.
PZ7.R761Wdi   1982   [Fic]   81-20502
ISBN 0-380-57158-7   AACR2

Printed in the U. S. A.

DON   10 9 8 7 6 5 4 3 2 1

Contents

The Pinto Colt

"IT DOESN'T look as if Uncle Torwal had come back yet," Whitey remarked to his cousin Josie as they stopped their horses on the high shoulder of Eagle Butte, overlooking the home ranch.

"There's no sign of his horse in the corral," Josie agreed. "Maybe he had to dig out Cedar Springs again. He said yesterday the water there was getting awfully low."

For almost as long as they could remember these two had lived here with Uncle Torwal on Rattlesnake Ranch, helping with the rough housekeeping and doing regular chores around the place. Riding here and there about various small jobs on the surrounding ranges, they more or less lost sight of the fact that they were considerably less than full-sized ranch hands.

Today they'd taken their lunches and made a long circle to the south, nearly to Elk Creek, checking on the springs and water holes. The long drought had dried up many of the watering places so that the few that were left had to be closely watched if the range stock was not to suffer.

Letting the horses rest now, they slouched in their saddles, admiring the view. From this high place they could see the windmill and the corrals casting long late afternoon shadows across the flats below. And the wild sunflowers growing on the dirt roof of the ranch house caught the sun, making a small bright patch of color above the weathered gray walls.

Long lines of cattle from the home range were strung out along the winding paths that fanned out from the troughs at the windmill. The thirsty ones, going toward the water, moved with a steady, purposeful gait, while the others, returning to the dry grazing beyond the ridge, idled along in scattered leisurely formations.

"Maybe we have time to practice roping some of those calves," Whitey suggested.

"I don't think we'd better," Josie disagreed as she slapped a fat horsefly off old Eagle's neck. "You remember what Uncle Torwal told us last time we did that."

"Guess he was right," Whitey answered. "With the range so dry they do get plenty of exercise just traveling to water, without our running any more fat off them." And nudging Spot's ribs with his heels, he woke the old horse from his drowsing and led the way down the slope towards the ranch.

At the stable they unsaddled; then, after leading the horses to the windmill to drink, turned them loose in the corral. It was still too early to start the supper chores, so they perched on the top rail to enjoy the cool evening breeze that was just springing up. After they had idled there a while, watching the

horses rolling in the deep dust, Uncle Torwal came in sight, riding slowly across the
sagebrush flat.

"There's something awfully queer about
the way he's riding," Josie said. "And there's
a horse following him, or else he's leading
it."

"It's the old pinto mare!" Whitey exclaimed, squinting against the low sun. "And he's got something slung across the saddle in front of him, too. That's why he's riding so carefully."

"You don't suppose it's a man, do you?" Josie asked, uneasily.

"No, silly! It looks more like a colt—let's go and get the gate open for him."

Scrambling down from the corral fence, they hurried past the windmill and were waiting at the pasture gate when Uncle Torwal rode up. As he came closer they could see that it was the pinto's colt he was carrying.

"What happened to him?" Whitey called. "Is he dead?"

"Some more of old Clubfoot's work," Uncle Torwal answered him, riding into the ranch yard. "Shut the gate and help me lift him down."

"You mean he's been wolf bit?" Josie wanted to know.

"That's right," Uncle Torwal told her. "I found them over on Antelope Creek. The ground was all tore up where the old mare had fought the wolf away. She's marked up a little, but not enough to do any damage. The colt is hurt worse, but I think we can fix him up."

While they talked the colt lay flat on the ground, making no effort to get to his feet. But as soon as Uncle Torwal moved close to him the old mare came up in short threatening rushes—snorting, stamping, and popping her big yellow teeth.

"Looks like we'll have to shut her up before we can do any doctoring," Uncle Torwal decided. "Open the corral gate while I get a rope on her."

After Whitey had swung the big gate wide and then scuttled to where Josie was already sitting on the top rail, Uncle Torwal climbed back into the saddle. Taking down his rope, he shook out a small loop and dropped it over the mare's head. Snubbing her as close as possible without getting bitten, he dragged her, squalling and fighting, into the corral. As soon as she was safe inside, Whitey scrambled back down and swung the gate shut while Uncle Torwal shook the loop loose and flipped it off her neck.

Finding she was shut in, the old mare ran up and down, whinnying and crying out between attempts to climb the stout fence while Uncle Torwal squatted on the ground outside to examine the colt's hurts. There was a deep, ragged gash on one haunch, and others over the ribs and on one shoulder at the base of the neck.

These had to be trimmed and cleaned to prevent festering. So while Whitey and Josie held the colt down, Uncle Torwal took his sharp knife to cut away the torn bits that would interfere with proper healing. Besides these wounds, there were a dozen or more deep round punctures in the colt's flesh.

"Fang marks," Uncle Torwal remarked. "Places where the old wolf struck with his tushes but didn't get a grip."

They carefully searched out each of those places and poured the peroxide into them until it foamed and overflowed onto the colt's hide. The big gashes were treated the same way, and then daubed over with a thick coating of lard and sulphur.

When these things had all been taken care of they lifted the colt to his feet and, while Whitey opened the corral gate a crack, Uncle Torwal pushed him inside. The colt was unsteady on his feet and, after nursing for a little, he lay flat on the ground again, at the old mare's feet.

"Do you think he'll get all right?" Josie asked as they peered between the poles to where the old pinto was standing guard over the colt along the farthest side of the corral.

"I imagine so," Uncle Torwal told her, "unless blood poisoning sets in from some deep bite we didn't get cleaned. Now, let's go wash up and get some supper."

As they went about their chores, helping cook supper and later cleaning up the kitchen, Whitey and Josie talked quietly about the wolf. This wasn't the first they'd seen of his work. He'd first showed up in Lone Tree County nearly a year before. Where he'd come from no one knew, for wolves had all been trapped out of the country years before.

At first he'd killed only an occasional calf or colt on what appeared to be simply trips passing through this range on the way to some other. But in the last months the kills had become more and more frequent until it was plain the big wolf had settled in the broken hills to the north.

As far as anyone knew, he never returned to a kill after his first meal from it. Because of this and the deformed foot that made his track so easily recognizable, it seemed probable that he had had considerable experience with traps—and perhaps with poison, also. At any rate, not even the professional trappers had been able to catch him in one of their sets. And month by month the record of his kills grew longer.

"It seems like somebody would catch that wolf!" Josie exclaimed fiercely, thinking of the gashes in the colt's hide.

"Yeah," Whitey agreed. "Something should be done about him, for sure."

"Just about everybody in the county has had a try at it, without any luck," Uncle Torwal reminded them. "Why don't you go after him yourselves? There's nearly two hundred dollars bounty on him by now." And, lighting the lantern, he went out to check on the windmill and turn the saddle horses into the night pasture.

"Maybe we'll do just that," they called after him.

At odd times during the next few days Whitey and Josie talked of ways they might

catch the outlaw wolf. They knew something of trapping, as they made extra money
every fall and winter catching muskrats and
skunks. And once they'd caught a coyote.
But they also knew that the big double spring
wolf traps were much too dangerous for them

to deal with. Besides, if the professional trappers had been unable to outwit the old wolf, it was a sure thing they'd have a poor chance. They'd have to think of something else.

"Maybe we could build some kind of deadfall," Josie suggested as they sat in the blacksmith shop looking at the badger's skin nailed up to dry on the back wall. "Like we did for the badger—only bigger, of course. It just might be that he knows about poison and wolf traps but wouldn't be afraid of a deadfall."

"Maybe," Whitey agreed, doubtfully, "or it might be we could catch him in a wolf pit, like the Indians used to do, if we dug it in the right place."

"Or, if that didn't work," Josie added,

"maybe we could set some sort of snare for him."

"I think maybe the wolf pit idea might be best," Whitey said, after some thought. "But first maybe we should dig one for practice to be sure we know how it is done. If we made one wrong and he got out of it he'd know all about such things and we'd never catch him again."

"That's a good idea," Josie agreed. "Maybe tomorrow we can try it."

By then it was time to start their chores. The pinto mare and her colt were still being kept in the small pasture with the saddle horses, and every day Josie and Whitey helped Uncle Torwal catch the colt to doctor his wolf bites. But the old mare still distrusted everybody, so each time Uncle Torwal had to rope her and put her in the corral before they could touch him.

"Why don't we turn her back out on the range and keep the colt here?" Josie asked Uncle Torwal one day.

"We've been talking about it," Whitey added, "and it seemed to us he's going to need a lot of care. We could sort of tame him at the same time."

"I think I see what you are really after," Uncle Torwal answered. "You want me to give you the colt, is that it?"

Well, yessir, they told him. He is a mighty pretty colt, and we could take care so nothing would happen to him like it might if we turn him back out.

For a while Uncle Torwal thought about that, then said, "He's still too young to wean, and if we keep both of them here you'll not be able to do any taming—the old mare will fight you every day. I think we'll turn them out on the range tomorrow." Before they could argue, he went on, "But you can ride out every day or two to keep an eye on him. Then this fall we'll bring him in and you can keep him here with the saddle horses if you like."

This didn't exactly suit them, but at least they had the promise of the colt for their own, if he lived through the summer. So now they were more determined than ever to catch the old wolf, to make sure he didn't get their colt.

The Wolf-Trapper

THE NEXT morning they hurried about their chores, washing up after breakfast, filling the wood box and the water buckets, making sure the water troughs at the windmill were full, and such things as that. Then they packed some sandwiches, took two shovels from the blacksmith shop, and saddled their horses.

"What do you figure to do today?" Uncle Torwal asked as he saddled his own horse,

getting ready to ride over to another ranch to
look at some calves.

"We thought maybe we'd go looking for
the old wolf," Whitey told him.

Uncle Torwal looked a little startled at

that, but all he said was, "Finally figured out a way to get him, have you?"

"Yessir," Josie answered. "We have a scheme that just might work."

"Well, if you find him don't let him get away!" Uncle Torwal said with a grin, and rode unconcernedly out of the ranch yard.

"I don't think he took us seriously," Josie said as she pulled her braids out from between old Eagle's big yellow teeth and finished yanking the cinch tight around his barrel chest.

"Just as well," Whitey answered. "He asked us and we told him. But if the story got round that we were really serious about catching that wolf we'd probably hear more than we cared to about it."

"I guess you're right," Josie agreed. "We'd better not say anything more about it until we catch him—if we ever do."

Riding out past Eagle Butte they began looking for a place to start their practice wolf pit. After inspecting and discarding several possible locations, they finally agreed on a deep-washed stock path leading out of a steep-sided draw. Dropping the horses' reins in a patch of high grass, they untied their shovels and got ready for work.

"How big should the pit be?" Josie wanted to know.

"It should be long enough so he won't accidentally jump over it and get away," Whitey told her. "About this long, I imagine," he went on, marking out a space about four feet long in the very middle of the path.

"We'll dig it deep enough so he can't climb out if he falls in. And after we've got it dug we'll put weed stalks across, then a layer of grass, and cover that with dirt so it looks just like the rest of the path. We might even make some cow tracks in the dirt, just to be sure and fool him."

"Won't he notice the pile of dirt we dig out?" Josie asked.

"I was just thinking about that," Whitey answered. "We'll unsaddle Old Spot and use the saddle blanket to carry the dirt away. That way there will be no sign of digging."

The bottom of the path was two or three inches deep in loose, dry dust, but below that the earth was packed almost as hard as stone. When they finally stopped to rest and eat their sandwiches, the wolf pit was no more than six inches deep.

"At this rate it'll take us until winter to dig a pit deep enough to catch a wolf," Whitey said, wiping sweat out of his eyes with his sleeve.

"Yes," Josie agreed. "And already I have two blisters on my hands."

For a while they sprawled on the grass, eating their sandwiches and saying nothing. They were so busy thinking about the problem of their wolf pit they didn't hear a rider coming from behind them until he spoke.

"Now that is an odd sort of place to dig a well," the stranger remarked, reining up his horse and leaning his arms on the saddle horn. "Or maybe it's for a cellar."

Looking up, they saw a small, scraggly sort of fellow on a scrawny, big-kneed horse wearing a beat-up looking old saddle. Lumpy sacks, apparently holding his gear, were tied onto his saddle with binder twine and, instead of boots, he wore plow shoes.

"It's a wolf pit," Whitey answered. "Or will be when we get it finished."

"Sounds like you were out after the bounty on the outlaw lobo," the disagreeable stranger said. "But if you have any such idea in mind," he went on, "you might as well give it up. I came out here especially to collect that scalp myself. And when Shorty Jarvis starts after a wolf he allus gets him."

Nobody answered him, and for a while the wolf trapper stared out over the country from under the droopy brim of his old hat. Then, spitting a stream of tobacco juice out over the old horse's already spattered shoulder, he rode away as quietly as he'd come.

For a while after he'd left there was nothing said. Then Whitey spoke up. "That must have been Shorty Jarvis," he remarked.

"Do you think he'll really catch old Club-foot, like he said he would?" Josie asked.

"I don't know," Whitey answered. "He talked big, but some of the best wolfers in the country have tried it before him."

"I know somebody should catch that wolf," she went on. "But it would seem more like we'd earned the colt if we could catch

him ourselves. Besides, if he tells about us digging a wolf pit we are going to look pretty silly if we don't catch him."

"Yeah, I know," Whitey agreed.

But, after talking the idea over some more, they decided to abandon the idea of trying to catch the wolf this way. In the first place, it was plain that digging a pit deep enough to hold a wolf from jumping out would be a bigger job than they could handle. Besides, there would probably be complaints from any ranchers or their riders who happened to ride into one of the wolf pits by accident.

"Anyway," Whitey decided, "a wolf that smart wouldn't go near a place where the ground has been fresh dug up, especially if there is man scent around."

"But neither one of us is a man," Josie objected.

"I meant people scent," Whitey patiently explained. "A wolf doesn't like the smell of people, no matter if they are big or small."

"Oh," said Josie.

A few nights later, as he and Josie were clearing up after supper, Whitey had another idea.

"That old wolf must sleep somewhere during the day," he said. "If we could just find the place we might catch him in it."

"Does a wolf like that make a den or does he just bed down out in the open?" Josie asked.

"The wolf hunters used to dig pups out of dens in the spring," Whitey told her. "And the Badlands over across the river are full of little caves and washouts that would make good dens. Maybe he sleeps in one of them during the day."

"But how would we find his den, even if he had one?"

"He'd leave tracks going in and out, and we could look for those."

"But supposing we did find him, what would we do then?" Josie wondered.

"The cowboys throw a slicker or a jacket —anything with strong man smell on it—into the entrance when they find a coyote den. If the old one is in there she won't come out, and if she is outside she will not go in to carry the pups away. So whatever was inside will be there when the men come back with shovels to dig them out. It should work the same way with a wolf."

From then on all their spare time was spent exploring the broken country beyond the edge of the breaks. It was a place full of cut-banks, washouts, and deep gullies, where almost any overhang might hide the entrance to an old den. And in many places the water, running off the eroded slopes in rainy times, had managed to find its way under instead of over obstructions, forming caves and grottoes of various sizes. Some might be no more than short natural culverts connecting one wash-out with another. Other times an entrance hole no larger than a rabbit burrow might lead into a series of small caverns connected by narrow winding galleries.

Day after day Whitey and Josie patiently searched these places out. Every lonely gulch or draw had to be carefully inspected. Many of the holes they found were obviously un-used. Others showed signs of use, but by packrats, weasels, skunks and other small creatures—not by wolves.

Just what sort of place the old wolf would pick, they did not know. It was possible, they knew, that he simply bedded down in some thicket of buckbrush or chokecherry. But nonetheless, each time they found what might possibly be a den they cautiously and quietly explored the surrounding territory from as far off as possible.

Much as they wanted to find the wolf, the last thing they wanted was to meet him face

to face in a narrow washout. After they had
made sure there was no movement to be seen
around the entrance of the den or anywhere
in the neighborhood, they would leave their
horses and move cautiously forward. Look-

ing carefully for any sign of tracks, or a hair caught on a bush, or even a rubbed place on a bank that might tell of the wolf's having been there, they examined the ground inch by inch. But always the result was the same. After finally looking into the dark entrance itself, they would decide that the wolf was not there.

They must have found and discarded hundreds of possible wolf dens without finding what they were looking for. However, they did come across several more of the old wolf's kills.

Occasionally they saw the wolf trapper in the distance, and once they came onto a coyote caught in a trap that had simply been hidden under the deep dust of a stock path.

But as far as they could tell, the trapper was having no more success than they were.

To make sure that their colt was still safe, they managed to ride within sight of the old pinto mare and her band almost every day. The colt's wolf bites had healed without crippling him—some scars showed here and there, but they were hardly noticeable on his spotted coat.

"Do you think he'll remember us when we bring him back to the ranch this fall?" Josie asked one day as she and Whitey watched the horses grazing quietly on a little flat below them.

"Most likely not," Whitey said. "But bright as he is we shouldn't have any trouble gentling him."

Smoke

"YOU FELLOWS want to ride to town with me today?" Uncle Torwal asked one morning as they stood on the ranch house porch watching the sun come up red through a haze that had hung over Lone Tree County for the last week.

"No, sir. I don't think I'll go," Whitey answered. "There are some things to do here. This would be a good day to put a headstall on the little hackamore noseband we braided for the pinto colt. It won't be long until we'll be able to bring him back to the ranch."

"Besides, that Stockmen's meeting will take all day," Josie added, "and there won't be anything for us to do but hang around waiting."

"Well, I guess you're right," Uncle Torwal agreed and picked his fancy town bridle off a peg by the door.

Whitey and Josie finished clearing up and washing the breakfast things, then hurried out to the corrals to watch Uncle Torwal saddle up. Almost everybody for miles around would be in town for the meeting, but they were used to being alone at the ranch. Besides, this would give them extra time to search for the old wolf's den, after they finished the hackamore.

"Don't forget to carry some wood into the kitchen and clean the ashes out of the stove before you get busy on other things," Uncle Torwal told them as he smoothed the blanket on his horse's back. "And if you have time you might grease the windmill. I notice it's been squeaking lately," he added. "But be careful."

"We won't forget," Whitey told him. "And we'll keep a lookout for prairie fires, too."

"That smoke is probably coming from the big forest fires out in Oregon or Washington," Uncle Torwal said.

Whitey knew this, but he still liked to imagine that there was danger of the nearby ranges catching fire. He'd never seen such a

thing happen, but he'd often heard the stories the old-timers told of lines of fire twenty
miles long sweeping across the country. And
it was a fact that Uncle Torwal and everybody
else in that country plowed wide fireguards
around their buildings and pastures just in
case such a thing did happen.

"The country is awfully dry," Whitey in-
sisted. "So we'll keep a lookout anyway."

"Whatever you think best," Uncle Torwal
agreed. Stepping into the saddle, he turned
his horse and brought him to the gate.

"Well, so long," he said, and rode out
towards the town of Lone Tree.

For a while Whitey and Josie were busy.
They carried wood to fill the woodbox beside
the old kitchen range, and argued about

whose turn it was to clean out the ashes.

When those jobs were finished they simply idled on the steps for a while, enjoying the quiet morning. And then they got out the special noseband they'd braided, some hackamore rope, and strips of old boot leather for brow-band and lacings. For a couple of hours they worked steadily at the complicated measuring and knotting involved in making the fancy rope headstall.

During the days before, they had paid little attention to the smoke but somehow, now that they were alone on the ranch, they couldn't get the idea of fire off their minds.

As they worked, they kept glancing at the haze beyond Eagle Butte. At times it seemed to them that it was getting thicker. Then it

would seem to thin out and almost disappear.

This time of year the grass everywhere was tinder dry, and already there had been several big fires on ranges to the south. Other fires had been burning for weeks in the western forests, hundreds of miles away, and sometimes the smoke from them would hang for days over the prairie country. But even so, Whitey and Josie grew more and more uneasy, and spent much of their time trying to decide if the haze was thickening. Somehow or other they had lost all interest in riding out to look for the old wolf.

"Let's go and grease the windmill and see if we can see anything while we are up there," Whitey suggested along in the middle of the morning.

Carefully climbing the old tower with the can of gear grease, they perched on the small platform at the top and looked around. From that height they could see for a long distance in all directions. But nowhere was there anything that looked like the kind of smoke that would mark a fire. But neither was there any sign of people moving–anywhere. Usually from the tower it was possible to see little dust columns stirred up by horsebackers going here and there about their affairs. So if a fire did break out it would only be a little time until help came from all directions. But today everyone in the county was in town, and probably would be until late in the afternoon.

"I guess Uncle Towal was right," Whitey remarked doubtfully as they climbed back down from the high perch. "It's just smoke from the forest fires."

At noon time, instead of fixing biscuits to go with the ham and gravy they'd planned on having, they each got a couple of cold flap-jacks and some cold bacon left from breakfast and hurried back outside to eat. The smoke didn't seem to be getting thicker, but still they were restless and found it hard to settle down to any of the little jobs that needed to be done.

The Prairie Fire

IT WAS EARLY in the afternoon when the thing they'd dreaded happened. A big fuzzy yellowish-white cloud suddenly began to boil up high into the sky from somewhere beyond the ridge to the west. It appeared to be several miles off, probably on the Elk Creek side of the ridge. The fire had most likely been burning slowly through short grass and buckbrush and had suddenly blazed up, to make the bigger smoke cloud that was rapidly growing.

55

There was no wind, but a fire that size would soon make its own draft and begin moving faster.

Earlier in the summer, Whitey had helped Uncle Torwal plow fireguards around the ranch buildings and around the fenced yards on the flat where the winter's hay was stacked. These were only plowed strips, four or five furrows wide. They served to stop creeping lines of fire until the fire fighters could deal with them, or as a base for the backfires that were sometimes set to meet an oncoming line of fire and starve it out. But by themselves the fireguards were no great protection; for a fire with a fair wind behind it could easily jump across them.

On all sides of the ranch the grass just outside the fences had been grazed off short, but in the big winter pasture running nearly to the tip of the ridge on the side next the fire the grass was nearly knee high. If a spark once got into that, nothing could save the ranch buildings or the stacks of winter feed.

"Do you think it'll come this far?" Josie asked as they uneasily watched the thickening smoke beyond the ridge.

"It's hard to tell," Whitey answered. "Depends on where it is. It may not be as close as it looks."

After another look all round in the hopes of seeing a dust coming from the direction of town, they saddled their horses and rode out to where they could get a better look. From the top of the ridge they could see the fire itself. Its blackened path stretched half a mile wide up the farther side of Boxelder Valley and disappeared over the ridge beyond. In the brush and high grass along the little creek the fire had spread out in both directions. And now it was working its way into the rough gullies and buttes between the creek and the foot of their ridge.

"Hadn't we better go after Uncle Torwal?" Josie asked. "That looks like it was coming right this way."

"By the time we went to town and back it would have time to burn the whole ranch out," Whitey answered. "Besides, the way it is going now, the fire may cross the ridge down yonder beyond our pasture."

"And there's no grass to speak of down on

the flats by the river," he went on. "So if it does that it'll burn itself out without doing any damage."

"Could we fight it ourselves?" Josie asked.

"It's too big for that," Whitey said. "But we can watch for blowing brands or burning tumbleweeds that might set the pasture on fire. If the wind doesn't come up from the

wrong direction we may be able to keep it away from the pasture and save the hay and buildings."

So they rode back through the gate and down to the ranch. At the windmill there was an old stoneboat with a barrel of water already on it that was kept there for such emergencies.

Whitey told Josie to carry gunny sacks and old pieces of canvas from the blacksmith shop while he got a bucket and filled the barrel to the top.

"One barrel of water isn't going to put out a fire like that one," Josie complained.

"We don't pour water on it, silly," Whitey told her. "Wait till we get back on the ridge and I'll show you how it's done."

Throwing the sacks and canvas over the top of the barrel to keep the water from splashing out, he fastened the rope from the stoneboat to his saddle horn and shook Old Spot's reins.

The old horse grunted and complained at the weight of the load dragging behind him in the dry dust of the yard. But after they got onto the grass, the going was easier and they

made good time. As they rode, they anx-
iously watched the smoke. Sometimes it
thinned out to an almost invisible thread, and
then again it would suddenly billow up in
great greasy fat clouds.

At the pasture gate they unhitched the

rope from the sled and tied their horses to the fence. Fishing around in the barrel, they each got a wet sack and hurried on up to the top of the ridge. A mile away the fire was working its way out of the creek bottom in two great horns more than a quarter of a mile apart. And between these big loops a dozen small fires, set by blowing brands, flickered slowly through the short grass.

The smoke was growing thicker, and occasionally a puff of hot air would drift up the slope towards them. But for now there was nothing to be done.

"Isn't it kind of dangerous for us to be here?" Josie wanted to know. "Suppose the wind changed and the fire came faster–right towards us–what would we do?"

"Fire wouldn't burn very fast here," Whitey explained, pointing out the hundred yards of close cropped grass, criss-crossed by deep worn stock paths between them and the fence. "If the wind did change all we'd have to do is get the horses and ride down to the river."

And for a while they watched the creeping lines of flickering red in the smoke-filled draws below them.

Small birds came darting out of the smoke, and a flock of sage chickens flew in dazed, heavy fashion just above the ground. Passing within a few feet of where Whitey and Josie stood, they set their wings to plane down the slope into the pasture. Jack rabbits, too, came up from the direction of the fire. Almost invisible in the dun-colored smoke, they moved past as silently as shadows and disappeared in the high grass after the birds.

"Look!" Josie suddenly exclaimed. "Aren't those horses down there?"

Looking where she pointed, Whitey could make out nothing at first, then through a rift in the drifting smoke he saw something moving on a little flat below. A little longer and he was able to make out the shapes of horses.

"It's the old pinto mare and some others," he said.

Beyond the horses the brush along the creek made a solid line of fire, while on either side of them the two other lines were burning their way up the slope along the bottoms of brush-filled gullies.

"Why don't they come on up here?" Josie wanted to know.

"They are afraid to pass those small patches of fire," Whitey told her. "If we don't do something about them they'll probably keep right on milling around down there."

"But how can we get them out?" she asked. "We can't go down there after them!"

"First we'll take care of enough of those spots to make a clear path they can see."

Hurrying back to the fence, Whitey had Josie open the pasture gate while he hauled the biggest piece of canvas out of the barrel where it had been soaking, and tied a corner to the end of his rope. Excitement and the smarting of his eyes made him clumsy, but he finally made his knot secure. Then, after

he and Josie had both tied wet handkerchiefs over their noses and mouths, he mounted Old Spot, who was nervously rolling his eyes at the thickening smoke.

Once in the saddle, he checked to make

sure that the other end of the rope was secure around the saddle horn. Telling Josie to bring a couple wet sacks, he fought the old horse's head around to face the fire. Drumming his heels and using the reins for a quirt, Whitey urged the old horse down the hill. Zigzagging this way and that to drag the wet canvas over the burning patches, he crossed and recrossed the line of scattered fires.

When the old horse refused to face the smoke any longer, Whitey dismounted. After taking Spot's bridle off and hanging it on the saddle horn, he turned him loose to go back to the pasture.

Snatching up one of the wet sacks, he ran to where Josie was beating out small patches of fire. The dragging canvas hadn't entirely smothered the burning places, but had broken them up into small individual fires that moved more slowly than the larger lines. The heat seared their faces, and now and again they had to beat out sparks that settled on their clothes. But in a few minutes the last small blaze had been put out.

"What do we do now?" Josie asked, as they looked about them.

"We'll go down and try to haze those horses up this way," Whitey told her.

As they made their way down to the flat through rolling clouds of yellow smoke, Josie suddenly stopped and pointed.

"That looked like old Clubfoot! I just got a glimpse of him as he ducked into one of those gullies!"

"Sure it wasn't a jack rabbit or a coyote?"

"I've seen coyotes," Josie retorted, "and this was bigger!"

"Well," Whitey said, "we haven't time to do anything about him now. Let's get on after the horses."

"But isn't it sort of dangerous to go on down there if the old wolf is there?" Josie asked.

"All he's thinking about is getting away from the fire. Let's get busy."

Down on the flat they saw old Pinto with her colt and five or six other horses, tightly bunched, milling restlessly about in the smoke.

Going quietly past them, Whitey and Josie turned, waving their hats and shouting, trying to drive the horses up the hill. But time after time, just as they reached the still smoking burned spots, the horses would break back and gallop heavily back to the imagined safety of the flat.

"Let's not hurry them this time," Whitey finally suggested. "Give them time enough to look that place over and they may find they can go between the burned spots."

And that time, after much snorting and looking, the old mare with her colt running close by her side broke from the ridge, weaving in and out between the rising plumes of smoke. Seeing her go, the others followed in a compact bunch. In the confusion one horse was crowded to the edge of a deep gulley, and a huge section of cut-bank caved from under his feet. For a minute it looked as though he would go down with it, but with a frantic lunge he got his feet onto solid ground and soon disappeared over the ridge to safety with the rest.

Whitey and Josie followed as fast as they could, glad to get out of that dangerous place. When they reached the fence they saw that all the horses had gone through the gate into the pasture.

"Well," Whitey croaked as they sat to rest with their backs against the cool wetness of the water barrel, "we finally got the colt home."

"Yes," Josie agreed. "Now if we can keep a spark from setting the pasture afire everything will be all right."

But as she spoke a sudden gust of wind swept up over the ridge, bringing with it a flaming tumbleweed. The big weed was rolling and bouncing straight for the pasture fence, and the high grass beyond—scattering small blazing pieces behind it.

Picking up wet sacks, Whitey and Josie ran and stumbled after it. Swinging the sacks, they tried to pin it to the ground. But it bounced this way and that over the rough ground and each time they missed it by inches. Just as it seemed sure to escape them, the weed struck the fence and tangled itself for a moment in the barbwire strands. Before the wind could tear it loose Whitey had wrapped it in the wet sack, while Josie scrambled through the fence to beat out the sparks that were already beginning to smoulder in the high dry grass.

When they had made sure that there was no more danger they went back to the water barrel. While they were splashing water on their scorched faces and soaking their arms and hands, Uncle Torwal and a dozen neighbors rode up.

"Looks like you've had a busy time," Uncle Torwal remarked. "You all right?"

"Yessir," Whitey told him. "And we got the old pinto and her colt out of a pocket down on the flats."

"I saw them as we came up," Uncle Torwal told him. "And it looks like the ranch would have burned if you hadn't caught that tumbleweed when you did."

While they'd been talking, the neighbors had taken wet sacks from the barrel and scattered along the ridge.

"They can take care of everything now," Uncle Torwal decided, looking to where the men were watching the fire. "Let's go down to the house and fix those blisters."

That night, after the fire had burned itself out, the men gathered in the kitchen to eat and talk a while about the fire before going on home. Whitey and Josie answered dozens of questions, but neither of them mentioned seeing the old wolf.

"If it was him he probably got out of there while we were after the horses," Whitey told Josie later in the evening. "But we'll go take a look in the morning, just in case."

End of Old Clubfoot

AFTER THE chores were done next morning, they saddled up and without saying anything to Uncle Torwal rode up over the ridge. For an hour or more they crisscrossed the gullied slopes and the flat where Josie thought she'd seen the wolf. They carefully examined the dust inside the entrance of every hole that he might have gone into. They did find a porcupine that had been suffocated by the smoke, and a couple of dead rabbits, but no sign of the wolf.

79

Giving up the search after a while, they started back to the ranch. On the way they stopped to look at the place where the bank had caved from under the running horse.

"If that horse had gone to the bottom he'd have broken his neck or a leg, sure," Whitey remarked as they peered over the ten-foot bank.

"What's that sticking out from under the dirt down there?" Josie asked. "Looks like a badger's fur."

"It does look like fur of some kind," Whitey agreed as they scrambled down for a closer look.

Scraping away more of the loose dirt, they finally uncovered what was surely the bushy tail of some kind of animal.

"Maybe it's a coyote,"   Whitey said.

"And maybe it's the old wolf, after all!"
Josie told him.

"Whatever it is, he must have been hiding
in the washout when the horse caved the
bank down on him," Whitey agreed.

As fast as they dug away the dirt with their
hands, more rolled down from above. So
they decided to go back to the ranch for

shovels. Finding several horses tied to the hitchrack by the ranch house, they rode quietly around behind the blacksmith shop to avoid having to explain what they wanted with the tools.

Hurrying back to the washout, they dug busily for several minutes before they uncovered the rest of the tail. By now they were convinced, from the size of it, that it belonged to some thing bigger than a coyote. And then, when they'd finally reached one of the hind feet, they were really sure.

"Look at the size of that foot!" Whitey said. "It's bigger than any dog I ever saw. It's old Clubfoot for sure!"

Another half hour of feverish digging, and they were able to drag the entire carcass out from under the dirt and stretch it out.

"That's old Clubfoot all right," Josie squeaked. "See that front foot?"

"It's him all right," Whitey agreed. "And what a whopper! He must be five feet long!"

For a while they simply sat there staring at the dead wolf, and thinking about the bounty they would collect.

"Well," Whitey said later on, "let's take him home."

"Will we skin him first?" asked Josie.

"Let's take him just as he is," Whitey suggested. "Old Spot will haul him—Uncle Torwal often carries dead coyotes and deer on him, during hunting season."

Dragging their prize out of the washout was a big job, but they finally managed it.

Then getting him onto the horse presented another problem, for the wolf weighed only a little less than either of them. But with Whitey in the saddle hauling on the tail and Josie lifting from below, they succeeded in getting him across the saddle. Tying him in place with the saddle strings, Whitey slid to the ground to lead the horse.

When they came slowly into the ranch yard there were still several men standing around talking to Uncle Torwal, and the wolf trapper was among them.

"What in the world do you have there?" Uncle Torwal asked after a startled look at the load on Old Spot.

"We finally got old Clubfoot!" Whitey answered.

The men gathered round to unfasten the ties and stretch the wolf on the ground.

"Biggest wolf I ever saw," somebody said. "How did you catch him?"

"Well, we didn't exactly catch him," Whitey admitted, and explained what had happened. "But we've hunted him all summer."

"Well, one thing's sure," somebody else said, "he won't kill any more colts."

"Do you think we'll get the bounty, anyway?" Josie asked.

"Sure you'll get the bounty," several voices said at once. "You brought him in."

"That ain't the way I see it," the wolf trapper said, shouldering his way roughly into the circle. "I been after him all summer, myself. And I'd probably have caught him if it hadn't been for these kids messing about all the time."

"Besides," he went on, "they didn't really catch him—they just picked him up dead. So it looks like he should belong to me, being as wolfing is my business, and after all the time I put in."

For a while nobody said anything, and Whitey and Josie waited to see how it would come out.

"Our Stockmen's Association offered a reward for the wolf's scalp because he was a killer," a rancher said after a bit. "And nothing was said about how he was to be caught. I think whoever brought him in is entitled to the bounty."

Everybody but the trapper agreed, and
before he could argue more, another rancher
spoke up. "While we are about it," he said,

"we've been looking for the place where that fire started yesterday and it looks like somebody had left a campfire smouldering and it got away. You were the only man out on the range yesterday—everybody else in the county was at the meeting in town."

"How was I to know the wind would fan that fire up?" the trapper mumbled after a little. "It looked like it was out when I left it."

And, without saying any more, he climbed on his old horse and rode away.

When he'd gone, the men skinned out the wolf's scalp, leaving the tail and deformed foot attached, and tacked it to the blacksmith shop wall to dry.

"Bring it to town at the next Association

meeting," one of the ranchers said, "and you'll get the bounty all right."

"Bear Paw Smith will want to show this skelp in his store," another said. "People will come for miles around to see it, so maybe you can trade him out of some trappings for that purty colt."

"We'll try it, anyway," Whitey answered.

For a while the men stood about telling each other wolf stories. Then, one by one they caught their horses and rode away while Whitey and Josie hung over the horse pasture fence admiring the pinto colt.